This book is dedicated to my wife Marjorie, my father Jean Andre Seignon, my mother Vasthie, my brother Marconi and his wife Sanderline, my sister Eunice and her husband Youri Pierre, my father in law Fritzner Michel, my mother in law Francoise Annette Michel and my nephews Samuel and Daniel.

Cover: Chris Marvens

The adventures of Uncle Bouki

Chapter 1

The Devastating Earthquake   8

Chapter 2

An Encounter with a Stranger   13

Chapter 3

Off to a New Start   18

Chapter 4

Meeting with an Old Friend   22

Chapter 5

Welcome to Sao Paulo   26

Chapter 6

Bouki meets Mr. Ventura   29

Chapter 7

Bouki gets the job   35

Chapter 8

Bouki and Lorenzo meet George Beret			40

Chapter 9

And the friendship ended				45

Chapter 10

Moving to Rio de Janeiro				54

Chapter 11

FIFA World Cup, 2014				57

Chapter 12

Making Traveling Plans				62

Chapter 13

America—Here I Come				66

Chapter 14

There is no ending to Bouki's Troubles		72

Chapter 15

Deported!   76

Chapter 16

The Borlette   81

Foreword

The human story of conquest and migration is woven into the fabric of the small but resilient island nation of Haiti. From Colombus' "discovery" of Hispaniola and barbaric genocide of its Arawak natives, to the pillaging of its land through the African slave trade; through French colonialism and revolt, to an independent Haiti wrought with dictatorships and natural disasters, the Haitian people have endured great hardships; yet they remain a proud and steadfast nation.

Since the establishment of the Western Hemisphere's first black republic, Haiti has had a long history of migration and temporary sojourn. As case manager for a refugee resettlement agency offering support to these Haitian sojourners, I have heard newly arrived Haitians tell of their long and arduous journey to the US. Their stories are sobering. Many fled to Brazil with great expectations following the 2010 earthquake, only to receive a less than warm welcome. The Brazilian government boasted a compassionate foreign policy to bring in more Haitian immigrants, but once they arrived no cohesive public policy was in place to properly receive them. A huge influx of Haitians came to Brazil seeking refuge and job opportunities, and instead discovered a country in economic crisis, wrought with rampant unemployment and anti-immigrant attitudes fueled by racism. A great number of these Haitian immigrants turned then to America's "lamp of liberty," and set out northbound. Many continue to travel thousands of miles on foot and by bus, through the Amazon and Andean wilderness, through the violence and upheaval of Central America and Mexico, facing hostility and confusion at each border crossing.

They survive off of each other and the occasional generosity of strangers. It is a remarkable voyage, and yet another example of the miraculous resiliency of the Haitian people, and of the human spirit.

As America watches the seventh anniversary of Haiti's catastrophic earthquake pass mostly unnoticed, the Haitian diaspora living among us finds itself at a crossroads. Where Haitians fleeing the devastation and abject poverty of their homeland once found refuge in the US, many are now confronted with the ugly reality of an unreasonable and broken immigration system. Haitians who only months ago were granted humanitarian parole and the right to work and rebuild their lives, are now facing indefinite detention at the border and summary deportations. It is yet to be seen how the current administration will handle the Haitian question.

The story of Haitian migration is not, however, one of unrelenting sadness. Many achieve great success here and obtain the skills and connections needed to return to their country and rebuild it. The grief carried by a character like Bouki is not exceptional, but his determination to remake his life and his homeland is. The difficulties facing Haiti are many, but the progress that continues to be made is happening thanks to the determination of individuals like Bouki, who harness the sense of community that lives on in the Haitian diaspora and return to their homeland.

Bouki faces the dilemma that all displaced persons are faced with: what to do with this new life in a strange land, and how best does one use the strengths God gives him to serve the people and place of his birth? At a time when the world faces an unprecedented refugee crisis, we ought to all heed the lessons learned from the Adventures of Uncle Bouki.

Ryan C. Smith

10 May, 2017

Chapter 1

The Devastating Earthquake

In the year 2010, a fearsome earthquake that shook the core of the country struck Haiti. It claimed the lives of thousands of people and many more were left homeless. This was not the first time the Caribbean country had faced a disaster. In fact, Haiti has never been alien to the misfortunes that any natural calamity is liable to bring with its arrival. Back in the days when Haiti was a French colony, many French historians had reported several cases of natural calamities including storms, cyclones, and earthquakes. The country has an element of unpredictability that is unmatched by any other.

In the South of the country, there is a city by the name of Aquin. It is part of a region on the south coast of Haiti. Beautiful yet poverty stricken, the area exudes an unparalleled charm and splendor. Living an ordinary life on this unpredictable land was Ti Jan Bouki.

Bouki was a lanky man nearing his 50th birthday. He was thin to the point of looking undernourished except for his small pot of a tummy. It seemed really odd for a tall and thin man to harbor such outgrowth. The little kids in his neighborhood used to say that Uncle Bouki had buried all his wealth in there. It was an absurd idea, but to their little minds, it sounded perfectly plausible.

Bouki had a beautiful piece of land near the coast. Before the earthquake, he had been a happy man. He was not very rich but then nobody in his immediate surrounding really knew what wealth really was. Yet, he was not exactly poverty stricken like the majority of people inhabiting Aquin. Apart from the land he owned that generated a decent income, Bouki was the mayor of Aquin.

He was married to a beautiful woman who knew how to make him happy. He reciprocated her efforts and emotions with equal zeal. After spending a blissful life of 20 years as a couple, keeping each other happy had become second nature to both of them. The accomplishment of their mutual feelings was their daughter, Rosaline. She was 19 years old when the earthquake in 2010 ruined everything for everyone. Bouki could still conjure a vivid picture of that fateful event, if he wanted to, but he did not want anything to do with the quake and it's horrendous after effects.

They had been warned about the calamity the previous night. The news was everywhere. It was on the television and every single person was discussing it. Some of the practical ones had left their homes to go and sleep under the open sky. Others were not so wise. They thought it was a minor threat and would not do much damage. Not many could understand the gravity of the situation.

It was 12:20 A.M. on January 10, 2010, when Bouki had first pondered over the phenomenon of death. He could tell that it was serious and they could die. He was among those who were wise enough to think that for once, they would be safe under the sky instead of inside their homes. "Come on, Dilly", he had begged his wife in earnest, "Let's leave the house for now." Dilia was a large woman. She was almost as tall as he was and at least twice his girth. Moreover, she was a willful woman, and once an idea took root inside her head, it was impossible to get it out of there.

In short, there was no way to move her without her consent. For some reason of her own, she was adamant about not leaving her house only because there was a threat of an earthquake. Consequently, she did not care to make a reply to her husband.

"Dilly, what has gotten into you", this time his voice was betraying a shade of irritation, "Why are you being like that now when you had never said no to me ever before?"

"Take it as my first and last request, then, Boo", there was no contempt or even anger in her voice. Her calm tones soothed him to a great extent. Still, he looked miserably in the direction of his daughter.

Rosaline, that epitome of beauty, was silently sitting in the corner of the room. She had wrapped a scarf around her head in her characteristic way. It was all on her head, making her look even wiser than she already was.

He observed his only daughter for a while. She was a statue of tranquility and it vexed him to see the two members of his family being so nonchalant about a natural calamity, even though they had seen such events destroy the country so many times before.

He sighed and gave in. Everyone in the whole town was sleeping now, except him. He could not sleep, afraid that a tremor would engulf his existence in the next few seconds. Nothing happened though, and while it took him a lot of time to do so, he finally fell asleep.

Nothing happened, neither that night nor the next morning. The danger was still lurking though and it was after 4:00 P.M that the calamity hit the country. That is when the world shook around him and he lost all he had ever loved and cared for.

Standing on the coast now, Bouki could picture it all. Each event was being played in the waves that came towards him. He wanted the ocean to eat him up just as the earthquake had devoured his Dilly and Rose. Man against nature, he thought, the ultimate battle.

He knew he was not strong enough to win the war that nature had unleashed on him. He could not end it in the traditional way, where fighting was required. He knew only one way to tackle the problem and that was to escape. The angry waves had stopped and the serene body of water spreading in front of him looked more inviting than ever…

Chapter 2

An Encounter with a Stranger

Being the Major of the town, Bouki had many responsibilities towards his people. He knew that as long as he held an important position, he could not afford to be selfish. This was the only reason that had stopped him from giving up his life. However, as of late, his thought process was not straight enough and that rendered him unfit for the position. He could not even look after his land properly.

He was sitting in his office. It was a small room decorated moderately with minimal furnishings. There was a table in the centre of the room, covered with a thick woolen cloth of green color. On the table, there was a small flag of Haiti standing diagonally in a transparent cup. The blue and red flag with a white patch in the centre, showcasing the coat of arms had usually succeeded in enticing patriotic feelings inside his heart. It was not having any effect on him today, though. He was actually resenting how the empty office had not faced much damage while the place with living people residing inside had crumbled. He was so engrossed in his thoughts that he failed to acknowledge the presence of another person in the room.

"What do you suggest we should do to repair the damage done by the quake, Sir?", asked one of his subordinates. He had been standing there for a while waiting for the Major to speak but Bouki had remained silent persistently.

The senior had no answer to that question. The man standing in front of him was much younger than Bouki was. He had sustained a few injuries because of the quake but lost his mother to it and yet he was thinking much more clearly than Bouki had done even for one second in the past week of chaos. Even this chap would make a better leader than me, thought Bouki.

"What do you suggest?", he asked of the young man.

"I am sorry?", said the assistant. His tone suggested that he was thoroughly confused by Bouki's suggestion.

"I trust your decisions and I am making you in charge of the situation for now", said Bouki and left the room without another word.

Bouki was walking on the shore of the beach. It was now his favorite spot. Not many people would come that way nowadays and that suited him perfectly. He wanted a serene place to collect his thoughts. The seashore granted him that tranquility sometimes, but there were other occasions, when the forceful waves of the sea only intensified the war that was going on inside him. He had spent his days in this alternate cycle of good and bad ever since the earthquake had robbed him of his sanity.

Why, he kept on reflecting on this one question from different angles. I was happy, I had everything, and then this had to happen.

There were other times when he could not feel anything except guilt for not being able to help the victims or play any active role in the rescue process. He knew it was high time he should come to a conclusion and make a final decision and yet he could not make his mind up.

His therapist, who happened to be his maternal aunt as well, had simply given him the advice to get some fresh air. Initially he had discarded the idea as being absurd, extravagant, selfish, and unnecessary. However, after a long and heated argument, she was successful in putting her point across effectively. He was actually thinking of moving away but one major hurdle stopping him from doing that was money.

After his routine walk at the seashore, he was returning home when a stranger stopped him. Bouki looked at the man, trying to place him but his memory failed him. The man was tall and dark and his features were roguish. His receding hairline and strong jaw line made him look older than he actually was. His tall figure was well maintained and it looked as if he exercised daily. Despite having contrasting features that looked as if there was no way he could smile and look friendly; he was smiling. He almost succeeded at looking mildly pleasant. Bouki was still staring at the stranger who looked as if he was in a hurry to put his point across. When Bouki did not say anything to allow the conversation to begin, the stranger decided to take matters into his own hands.

"Look, I am from the neighboring city and I want to talk to the Major", said the stranger. His voice was husky and Bouki was still unable to comprehend what this man's purpose could be.

"Yes, that would be me", said Boukie, "What do you want?"

"They told me I will find you here", replied the man, "I am need of a piece of land around the area for agricultural purposes."

"What do you want to grow things here for?" asked the town head in a slightly rude tone. "I mean, the area is all damaged, you see, and I am not sure it is the right time for anyone to look for land", he tried again after witnessing the shock in the eyes of the other man at his rudeness.

"It is part of my project. I am trying to do something for every affected area of the country", explained the stranger, "However, I want to do it fast and this is why I thought the best way to do so was to come straight to you."

He was smiling now. It made Bouki thoughtful and he felt rather small for not doing anything for the others who were suffering at the hands of the earthquake. The country needed to pull itself together and rebuild itself. This was when Bouki made a final decision.

He decided to sell his own piece of land to this man as he knew that there was not much he could do to change the current situation of his town because of his own grief. It was becoming exceedingly difficult for him to control his distress anymore. Every part of the area reminded him of his family and that made him extremely sorrowful. He knew the best course of action for him was to get away from it all. "You will have your piece of land. Meet me tomorrow morning in the office", he told the man who nodded and left immediately.

Bouki returned to his home and went straight to his bedroom. There, he unlocked the upper shelf of his cupboard. He could see a few hundred gourds and the legal documents of his land. This was all he had—all that he and Dilly had saved. Originally, most of it was to be spent on Rose's education, but due to her untimely death, he was now free to use it all in whatever way he liked. He was going to use it for traveling!

Chapter 3

Off to a New Start

The next day, Bouki took extra care while dressing for the office. He wanted to impress the stranger and somewhat repair the damage his behavior from the previous day might have done. He looked all crisp for his meeting with the stranger. He had also packed the important documents in his briefcase. He was ready to follow his decision.

For the first time in the last week, he reached the office on time. He did not want to be late for the meeting either. He was faintly excited about this venture. The previous night, he could not sleep because he had been thinking about leaving the place. While that made him a little sad, he knew in the long run, it was a good decision that would help him grow and he definitely needed that. He knew that there was no point in living his life, stuck in the past. He was ready for his destiny that he knew awaited him with open arms, but in another country.

He settled in his office, waiting for the stranger to show up. However, minutes turned into hours and yet there was no sign of that man. Bouki felt really stupid and he was especially annoyed with himself for not bothering to ask for the stranger's name. It was half past 6 in the evening, there was no sign of the man, and that is when hopelessness started to engulf him. The depression attacked him anew. It had been a routine until now but today, the feeling attacked him suddenly and caught him unaware. This was overwhelming to a greater level and all his past difficulties, regrets, failures, and sorrows were upon him in the form of an army instead of slowly creeping upon him as was routine with him.

This had a strange effect on him and he was ready to commit suicide then and there. Yet he failed to move as the spirit in him, of which he was a staunch believer, stopped him from doing so. Paralyzed by the intensity of the shock that had just been delivered to him, he was sitting there in his office. One by one, all the pieces of his personality were being shredded and he could not do anything about it. This was when the door of his office burst open.

Given his present condition, it would have taken a huge of amount effort from him to just look at the newcomer but the urgency with which the stranger had burst into the room was enough to startle him into looking reflexively in that direction.

The man standing in front of him was none other than the previous night's apparition. Bouki realized that it had been ages since he had been happy to see someone. The stranger was smiling and Bouki tried to imitate that gesture too.

In the next 24 hours, everything was settled. The property was sold and the money had been transferred too. Bouki was all ready to move away from his hometown once and for all but only mentally. He had not yet decided which place he wanted to visit the most. Unable to decide which destination would suit him best, he decided to visit the cemetery.

He had no idea, which grave his Dilly and Rosaline had been buried inside. The casualties were vast and it was a miracle he was not lying with them. However, it was a miracle he was finding really hard to appreciate. It was all about the timing. Dilly had asked him to get some yogurt from the store only a few minutes before the calamity had struck. Therefore, he was out in the open. While he had felt his head spinning at the speed of light and immediately lost his balance, he had not received any dangerous injuries.

However, Dilly and Rose had not been so lucky. When they had fallen to the ground, the house and the surrounding buildings had followed course too. Therefore, they were found buried beneath the rubble and by the time the rescue teams had arrived to save them, their bodies were not even recognizable—such was the extent of the damage.

When Bouki had asked where the people from his residential area were buried, he was shown to a row of graves. Therefore, Bouki would just randomly walk along that row and communicate with his dead wife and daughter. They had never replied to his pleas, raging outbursts, or pitiful cries but he was not the one to be discouraged. Surprisingly, it was the one place that made him feel less lonely. However, there was no way he would be allowed to spend the rest of his life in the midst of a bunch of graves. After all, he was the Major. Not anymore, though, he thought. Before he came to the cemetery, he had taken care of that part.

He resumed his ritual of walking among the graves, using his spirit to find the spirits of his family. It took him awhile but by the time he was done, he had made up his mind as to where he was going to go!

The flight leaving for Brazil was ready and so was Mr. Ti Jan Bouki with all his luggage and memories from the past.

Chapter 4

Meeting with an Old Friend

The flight to his new destination was without any event. Everything was happening at a normal pace and despite this normality; Bouki could not feel normal at all. He was excited, apprehensive, as well as sad. He had no idea what the next stage of his life would bring for him. It was February 1, 2010 and he had chosen the date with extreme care. The date not only marked his 50th birthday but it also completed 20 years from when he had first met Dilly. The date was indeed special!

Bouki's flight landed in the capital city of Brazil, Sao Paulo. He had chosen the place not only because the spirits at the cemetery had told him to do so but also because he had a friend there. It was around 25 years ago when he had met Lorenzo Augusto. The man had traveled up to Aquin with some friends of his. They were on a mission to explore the world and this is when they had met Bouki, who was working in a bakery at that time.

Bouki was educated and had splendid ideas, which were loved and honored by Lorenzo and his friends. They stayed together for a short period of one week but it was enough to harbor a deep friendship between the two. Therefore, it was not a strange consequence that the first name that came into Bouki's mind when a calamity hit him and his family was of his friend Lorenzo's!

They had remained in contact for a while after their first encounter through letters and emails but soon it ended. Therefore, at first, Bouki felt rather indecisive about contacting his old friend. However, he was the only man he could truly trust in this state of emergency.

No doubt, Bouki had been successful in his career and had met several people in his life but he had learnt it the hard way that everybody was not to be trusted. As a result of his life's lessons, he only trusted his immediate family that was his wife and daughter. Since they were not there to vouch for him anymore, he knew only one other name that could help him with his current situation.

Before contacting his old friend, Bouki had investigated about him on his own. He had found out that Lorenzo's worldwide travels had been fruitful in at least one way. After moving from one country to another, he had settled in his own city and started working in the tourism industry. Bouki respected his friend a great deal for returning to his country even after visiting the whole world. He knew Lorenzo had been to all the amazing and wonderful places the world had to offer. He had seen many of his pictures.

Even when they were not in close contact, Lorenzo would send him a few pictures of his adventures after every excursion. This made Bouki smile each time he received a photograph of his friend. Every time, he received a mail, his heart used to skip a beat as he thought it might be from his dear friend. With every passing year, the bundle of photographs kept piling up and Bouki arranged them in an album form. It was around 10 years ago, when Bouki received a message from his friend informing him that Lorenzo had returned to his own country for good and he was planning to stay there for the rest of his life. Lorenzo had clearly stated that he wanted to work in his own country and Bouki had felt quite proud of his friend's motives.

Even though Bouki was going away from his country for now, it was only because he could not bear to look at his land, destroyed as it now was because of the devastating earthquake. His love for his country and hometown had never dwindled for even a second. He had been thinking these thoughts throughout his flight and it was only when he saw his friend waiting for him at the airport that he let go of his longing for the country and city where he had spent around half a century.

Bouki did not immediately recognize his old friend. However, it took him merely a few seconds to make out the twinkling blue eyes behind the mess of a beard. To his friend, Lorenzo looked shorter than his actual 6 feet height. It was because age had hunched his back a little, taking a few inches from his height. He was dressed in a grey suit. His full lips were curved in a smile and he was taking fast steps towards his friend, wanting to reach him as fast as he could.

Presently, he reached him and without waiting for the other to make a move, both of the old men grabbed each other into a warm hug. They stayed that way for a while and by the time, they broke the grasp and overcame their emotions; several other people had stopped to stare at this show of emotions. They looked a little embarrassed but happy nonetheless. Finally, they were ready to speak. "That is some beard you have grown there, Lo", said Bouki breaking into a smile, "What fertilizer have you used for such lavish growth?"

"This beard is nothing compared to the number of wrinkles on your old face", replied Lorenzo.

Both of them started laughing uncontrollably. It felt really good to be in the company of someone who could understand you, thought Bouki.

Chapter 5

Welcome to Sao Paulo

The journey from the airport to Lo's house was spent in the back seat of a taxi, where both friends caught up with what had been happening in the life of the other. While Lorenzo knew about the demise of Bouki's wife and daughter, he did not know the details of the event. Bouki had only informed as much to his dear friend in the letter that he had written only a few days ago. Therefore, it was only natural for Lorenzo to ask his friend more on the topic and while it would have been a painful task for him to recall the happenings of that unfortunate day in front of any other person in the world, it was different with Lorenzo.

It was only after the two had conversed on the topic in detail that Lorenzo started relating the story of his life. "I had been running all around the world as you know", said Lorenzo, "but when I turned 40, I realized that I was not doing anything fruitful."

"What do you mean by that?" asked Bouki. It was puzzling for him to hear his friend say that since even after so many years, he could still recall his friend's wanderlust. As far as Bouki was concerned, following one's passions was a fruitful endeavor on its own.

"Do not take me wrong. I loved what I did. In fact, I still do and whenever I get the time, I travel around a bit", replied Lorenzo, "But you know as fulfilling as it was, I could not bring myself to face the reality that I was living a very self-indulgent life."

This made sense to Bouki who respected his friend's decision. "So what do you do now?" asked Bouki.

"Well I have succeeded in turning my passion into my work, after all", said Lorenzo.

"How?" asked Bouki.

"I am into tourism", said Lorenzo, "Not only does that generate a good income for me, it is also a nice way for me to do something for my country."

Bouki looked impressed by the shrewd decision of his friend. "What is it that you do exactly?" he asked.

"A lot", said Lorenzo, "The company I work for, provides tourism packages for foreigners, covering everything from hotel stays, things to do here, and tours to famous places in Brazil, to providing affordable traveling deals as well."

"This is great", said Bouki, "Do you think there is any way you can fix me up at this job as well?"

"You got it, my friend", Lorenzo was laughing. Then he added, "The moment I had received your letter, I knew you would be here for a while. Therefore, I had been looking for a place to fix you up."

"How had you figured that out?" asked Bouki surprised.

"Your writing suggested that much. I am your friend and I can tell your feelings from your words. Even if it had been ages since we had met but your letters and replies to my pictures were enough for me to remember you and your ways", said Lorenzo with a smile on his face.

This made Bouki smile as well. "So what did you find for me?"

"You will be coming with me to the office on Monday but there are two solid days till then and that is enough time for me to show you my lovely city", said Lorenzo and Bouki noticed a hint of pride in his friend's voice.

Chapter 6

Bouki meets Mr. Ventura

Bouki and Lorenzo utilized the two days in the best way possible. The two friends did justice to the largest city in South America and traveled from one corner to the other. Their plan was to cover all the important places of interest as best as they could and they did just that!

Bouki found out a lot about the city including its unique location on the Piratininga Plateau. He realized that the place was surrounded by breathtaking rivers, which were fanning out in the interior. Lorenzo told him that ever since it was found in 1554, the famous city of Sao Paulo had become Sertao's gateway or Brazil's backcountry. He further explained that the explorers from the city that visited the region back in that time were called bandeirantes and the modern day highways moving towards the interior cities followed the same route.

Bouki observed that the city harbored a number of immigrants from various countries and each had touched the city's culture in their own characteristic manner. These influences came from Spanish, Portuguese, German, Jewish, African, Japanese, and Arab residents. The immigrants had left enough impression on the city, for it to be observed in the form of museums dedicated to the Japanese immigration and the Africans' contribution to Brazil. For Bouki, however, the most exciting part of traveling around this city was its sheer size. He could not help marveling at the beauty spread in front of his eye as the two friends climbed the 46-story Italia Building—AvenidaIpiranga.

Since they had to cover a number of tourist attractions of the famous city, all of which were widespread, they preferred traveling via Metro. Each night, they would return to Lorenzo's small apartment in the main city, tired from the day's excursion but happy and content.

While Lorenzo realized how much he was missing the company of a great friend like Bouki, the other man was simply glad to have an excuse to think of anything other than his destroyed city and lost family. It had been the first time after the quake had struck his city that he was genuinely happy and laughed a real laugh. He did not have to fake and pretend anymore. He was truly delighted with what was happening in his life.

The two of them had momentarily forgotten that they were 50 now and not 25 anymore. Their spirits were flying high and even when the weekend was at its final minutes, Bouki was still happy. He knew that from now on, he would be working instead of having fun with his beloved friend. Yet, it did not bother him at all. In fact, when he finally fell asleep, he realized that he was actually looking forward to the next day and its proceedings.

—

The next day, the morning was bright. The chill from the previous night had vanished and warmth was oozing from every corner of the clear sky. Despite being in a good mood, Bouki was still a little nervous. He could not help glancing in the direction of his friend after every few seconds as if just looking at Lorenzo would somehow transfer positive energy into him. Yet, no matter how many times, he would look at his friend the nervous feelings would not go away. Lorenzo kept smiling at his friend encouragingly. He briefed his friend all about his boss and his manners and the ways around his employees.

"You wouldn't believe how nice Mr. Ventura is, Bouki", said Lorenzo, "There is no way he would make you feel bad at all."

"It is not really about how Mr. Ventura is, or how he treats people", replied Bouki in an irritated voice. "The problem, my dear friend, is that I have no idea how to take orders from other people anymore."

After listening to this, Lorenzo was quiet for a while. He was thinking of a reply to give when Bouki started talking again.

"It's been ages since I have worked under someone. For the past 4 years, I had been working as a Mayor in my city and before that, I had my separate team who I was responsible for. All I ever did was make yearly reports to be submitted to the headquarters and they all trusted and respected me enough that there was never any trouble of any kind from that department."

Lorenzo listened to this long speech without uttering a single word. At last, he spoke, "I see your difficulty, my friend, but I still insist that you meet Mr. Ventura."Bouki smiled at him half-heartedly but nodded.

The office was on the 7th floor of the 10-floor building. Bouki observed the building with great interest. It had a minimalistic design, which was elegant in its own way. When looked at from the outside, each floor of the building had several windows, each of which was tinted silver. It gave a very grand look to the building. Both of them entered the building. There was a reception on the right corner but Lorenzo who was leading the way, did not stop at the reception, but kept moving to the centre of the building. Bouki followed him in complete silence. As they reached the centre, Bouki saw there was an elevator. They rode it and went straight for the 7th floor. By the time, they had reached the room, which was labeled "Amazonian Expedition", Bouki was sweating profusely.

Lorenzo glanced sideways at his friend. It was funny and yet pathetic to see a 50-year-old man losing his calm over something as petty as a job interview. However, it was not a small task for Bouki at all. He was planning to keep this job as his source of income for a while and he knew he needed money to thrive in this foreign land. Lorenzo had already done so much for him that it was extremely painful for Bouki to even think of asking for more. Therefore, it was essential for him to get this job.

Despite the urgency, it was not as if Bouki had not had thoughts of giving up on it several times. In fact, he had thought of returning to his country several times in the past few seconds but he knew there was nothing left in that direction either. Moreover, Bouki had never learnt to move backwards. He only knew one way to move and that was always forwards!

Immersed in such thoughts, Bouki followed his friend through the wooden door. There was another reception behind which a pretty girl was standing. She was smiling with a welcoming gesture that made her look even prettier. Bouki glanced around the little space, which had a lot of shelves and drawers. On glass panes, several brochures were arranged neatly. Lorenzo told him to wait at the reception and went through another door. This one was made of glass but the pattern on the glass made the texture hazy and therefore, it was difficult to know what was happening inside the office. Bouki looked around and saw a red sofa in one corner of the little space. He took a seat on it and started observing the brochures. They were all advertisements of affordable travel packages offered by "Amazonian Expedition." Bouki found them interesting. He peeked at the girl from the corner of his eye. She was busy sorting through the various brochures and did not take any notice of him. He busied himself with the brochures and then looked her way again after a few seconds. He kept repeating the cycle and then he saw her watching him. He averted his eyes in confusion. Then he dared to look towards her once again and found her smiling at him. This embarrassed him and he decided to not look in her direction at all.

"Are you a foreigner?", she asked.

He looked at her perplexed that she was addressing him. Then he nodded.

"Here for a job?", she asked kindly.

He nodded again. She smiled and wished him best of luck.

He tried to smile but it looked like a grimace.

He realized that the girl was not as young as he had initially thought. Yet, she would still be at least 20 years younger than he was. What are you thinking about, he reproached himself, also so soon after Dilly!

He pushed the thought away and presumed a stern look. He was almost calm when the phone on the reception desk rang. The pretty woman attended it and after a minute of conversation, she politely asked Bouki to go through the glass door and turn to the right, where Mr. Venture was waiting for him.

Chapter 7

Bouki gets the job

The room inside the office was tense. Bouki tried to calm himself down. He tried to focus on the most important part of the room, which was the man sitting on a seat behind the central desk. It took him a while to do so but he was finally able to concentrate.

The man offered Bouki a seat and he accepted it. Bouki focused on the man's face and his form. It was nothing like Bouki had imagined. In his mind's eye, Mr. Ventura was an old, thin, mean looking, white man. However, the man sitting in front of him was young, corpulent, friendly looking, and black. Upon further concentration, Bouki realized that the man was grinning.

Bouki found it extremely odd. He had worked for so many years and he had never met any person in a senior position with such a frank disposition. Mr. Ventura recognized the puzzled look on the newcomer's face. Apparently, he had seen it before as well. Therefore, it did not surprize him at all. Instead, he smiled at Bouki.

"You seem shocked to see a person in my position smiling", said Ventura smiling, "I can see you were expecting someone sterner?"

"Well not really", said Bouki, then added after a while, "I will admit, I was not expecting someone so young, though."

Bouki was thoroughly impressed to see that the man was so young and yet so successful.

"Age", said Ventura "is nothing more than a meaningless number."

Bouki just smiled in reply.

"Anyways, let's talk business…"

Ventura and Bouki talked for the next hour without anybody interrupting them, which was on Ventura's orders. It was a part of their company's policy and they took it very seriously. Everything was confidential and yet the man working behind it all was extremely polite and soft spoken. He asked Bouki several questions. Some of them were directed at his personality while others were asked to estimate Bouki's general knowledge.

Ventura especially tested his knowledge on geographical boundaries and tourism. Lorenzo had taught him enough on these subjects and Ventura was almost impressed. By the time the interview ended, Bouki was in high spirits. He had no idea if he was hired or not but just the experience of going through this process was thrilling enough for him. He was glad he had met this excellent man. They sent him home on that day and told him that he would get a call if he was selected.

When he came out of Mr. Ventura's office, Lorenzo was standing outside. Bouki wondered if his friend had been standing there, all the while Bouki was inside but then he decided it must not be the case since there was a lot of work to be done in the company and there was no way an important man like Lorenzo could spare an hour simply waiting outside Mr. Ventura's office for his friend. Pushing the thoughts away, Bouki advanced towards his friend and told him in whispers what had passed between him and Bouki inside his office. Of course, he was not entitled to spill the beans to another person especially an employee of Mr. Ventura's but there was no way he was going to not take his friend into confidence. He loved Lorenzo too deeply to allow a company's work policy to come between them.

Lorenzo kept nodding at every word he heard from his friend. By the end of their conversation, the two friends were standing outside the office building. They had unconsciously walked to that point. Lorenzo looked at his friend and smiled.

"Do not worry, my dear friend", he told Bouki, "Mr. Ventura is a man of principles and he would never deny this job opportunity to you."

Bouki smiled and then he said, "I am not worried. It is only that the man is so nice that I wouldn't want to miss a chance of working with him."

He then went home, taking the keys of Lorenzo's flat.

The rest of the day passed without event. Bouki cooked a delicious meal as he reached home and then he went straight to sleep. He was so tired because of all that happened in the day that there was no option for him but to lie down a bit. When he finally woke up, it was evening already and Lorenzo was home.

Bouki got up and went to talk to his friend. Lorenzo was sitting at the kitchen table, devouring delicious looking ravioli. He was gulping mouthfuls with a glass of orange juice. Seeing his friend eating his food so enthusiastically, Bouki realized how hungry he was too. Bouki grabbed a fork from the kitchen counter and started helping himself.

"Why didn't you eat what I had cooked earlier?" asked Bouki. He tried to look offended but it was apparent that he was only trying to tease his friend.

"A few friends came in while you were sleeping and I served it all to them", said Lorenzo, "but it was not much of a loss, considering what a pathetic cook you are."

Bouki just glared at him in silence. However, he knew that Lorenzo had only spoken the truth. Back at home, when they were alive, it was his wife and daughter who did the cooking. Before he was married, it was his mother and sisters. There was no question of his ever making a meal. Therefore, he had little to no experience in that quarter.

"It is ironic, though", said Lorenzo, "You used to work at the bakery and you do not know anything about cooking. Would you care to explain that?"

"You have no idea what I did at the bakery now, do you?" asked Bouki. It was somewhat sad to know that his friend did not remember his job description at the bakery, where he used to work at least 25 years ago.

"It was 25 years ago. Come on, is it not extraordinary that I could recall you worked at a bakery?" came the tantalizing response of Lorenzo.

"I was the delivery guy", said Bouki and he still looked a little angry with his friend. Lorenzo only smiled in response.

They kept eating in silence but then Lorenzo broke it.

"I hope you will not turn out to be as lousy at "Amazonian Expedition" as you are at the cooking."

Chapter 8

Bouki and Lorenzo meet George Beret

After Bouki got the job at "Amazonian Expedition", his time started passing by nicely. He loved the company of his friend and Lorenzo reciprocated his feelings with equal enthusiasm. They knew how to take care of each other. They looked after one another's interest at work and divided responsibilities at work. They had built a nice life there in the city of Sao Paulo.

They dated women even, but both of them knew that neither was going to go for a long-term relationship anymore and they had it all figured out. For three years, they spent a simple life saving each other's back. However, in the third year of their friendship, life decided to take a tragic turn that shook Bouki's life once more.

It was winters in Sao Paulo and Lorenzo was as careless about his health as ever. Bouki had tried to explain to him so many times that they were not 25 anymore, not even 45.

"Why don't you understand that we are not young people", Bouki had scolded his friend for the umpteenth time, "We are losing vigor. This is the painful truth and there is no point in denying it."

"I am not denying anything", Lorenzo had retorted. He was irritated by this continuous lectures offered by his friends. He was not done with life for now and there was no point he was going to stop living it until it ended on its own. He would tell his friend that he knew they were growing old but he was not ready to lose spirit.

"The spirit, and I am talking about your alcoholism here, is injuring you", Bouki had said. He looked dismal and many years older than his actual age. His beard was growing unchecked and the wrinkles on his face were deepening day by day. Yet, he did not look haggard and unhealthy like his friend did.

Lorenzo had grown extremely thin and his balding forehead was pushed backwards with the excess of wrinkles. Living the life at his own price was taking its toll on him and there was nothing Bouki was able to do to save his friend.

—

It had been in that last year of their friendship that they had met George Beret. This man was from Australia originally but he had settled in Brazil around 10 years ago. He was a middle-aged man with a dark beard and small eyes. He was in the business of construction and he had hit a huge fortune by investing his energies and talent in building the stadiums during the World Cup season. Ever since then, he had never returned to his country. He was a single man and extremely handsome. However, he did not have any intention of marrying anytime soon either. He had a few things in mind, which he needed to take care of.

Lorenzo and Bouki had met him at a party, which was thrown by their boss, Mr. Ventura. He was the only man wearing a suit and tie and his persona screamed that he was a businessman of some sort. Lorenzo had been extremely impressed by this young man and asked Ventura to introduce him to him. It did not take Lorenzo much time to charm George Beret. Before the poor guy had any idea what he was doing, he had invited Bouki and Lorenzo to pay a visit to his construction company.

"Which one are you talking about, Sir?" Lorenzo had asked. George Beret had several construction companies and only one of them was in Sao Paulo about which he was talking about.

"Obviously the one that is most convenient for you", he had replied.

The matter had been settled and they were to visit their new friend at his company in Sao Paulo. After the party, the two friends discussed the matter among themselves. While Lorenzo really liked the new man, Bouki had some reservations.

"He is an extremely wealthy man", said Bouki, "it is really hard for me to digest that type of wealth."

Despite seeing so much in his life, money was something Bouki still could not understand. The concept that a man should hoard a large fortune was not easy to fathom for him. Back at home in Haiti, he had always watched people struggle for even the basic necessities of life. For him, it was enough if a person could afford the basic provisions and the rest was just luxury.

Lorenzo was well aware of his friend's ideals and he could never bring himself to accept them. For him, money was a good thing and the more you had it, the better it was. So he retorted, "I know why you say that, Bouki, but you do realize that not everyone has the same ideas about money as yours. Some of us are still in awe of it because it helps us buy whatever we desire."

Bouki looked at his friend, who was definitely on the verge of being drunk. A feeling of disgust took over him and he started screaming at him.

"I can see all that your heart desires is to drink and drink, my friend, till you could drink no more", his voice sounded dangerous, coming at such a high pitch. It was perhaps the first time he had been so harsh with Lorenzo. This shocked his companion to an extent that he was left speechless for the time being.

However, before they could resume their fighting, Bouki thought it was best for him to simply leave the room.

There were times when they could keep on fighting like that for several days. It was in the midst of these fights that they went to visit the construction company of their new friend George Beret. Having a third person with them helped their relationship a lot as well. Soon, the three of them became rather great friends.

Chapter 9

And the friendship ended

With time, Bouki learned to accept George Beret for the person he was—a businessperson. For him, opportunities were of the utmost importance. He used to chase after them with all the energy he had and if there were no opportunities to be found, he was the type of man who knew how to create his own luck.

Bouki was definitely differently wired than this man but he could not help appreciate the other personality traits this man had, for George Beret was not a person of single passion. He was also compassionate and kind. He knew how to make friends and keep them too, and for Bouki, these were the most important qualities in any person. He, too, had those characters and in excess. Therefore, Lorenzo and his addiction considerably shook him. After a few months had passed, he decided to seek help to deal with the ever-increasing problems of Lorenzo and his first choice was George Beret.

One evening when the three of them were having their usual discussions, Lorenzo just passed out and Bouki decided that it was the best time for him to discuss the issues with their third friend. With George's assistance, he transferred his friend to the other room. They then sat in the dining room again over their own drinks which were nothing compared to their friend whose loud snores were now echoing throughout the house.

"I know you must have observed the troubles of our friend", said Bouki. His heart was racing, as he feared that Lorenzo might not be asleep and some scrap of their conversation would still be understandable to him. So, he continued to speak in a low voice.

George Beret only nodded solemnly. Apparently, George thought there was no hope but when Bouki kept on pestering him about it, he realized how serious he was. Bouki explained to him how dearly he thought of Lorenzo and how he had not been like that to begin with. George could tell their friendship was rather deep and they were more like brothers. It was definitely hard for one brother to see the other go down like that.

"I know of someone who could help us with Lorenzo's situation", George told Bouki.

This improved Bouki's spirits. He was now listening attentively to George, hanging on to every word he uttered.

"Well, it was a long time ago. I had an acquaintance and he had a similar level of addiction However, his wife took him to this famous rehabilitation center. While his recovery took some time but eventually, he started showing improvement", related Mr. Beret.

Bouki did not give an immediate reply but his eyes were shining with hope. He had finally seen a silver lining and only he knew for how long he had waited for it. After his overwhelming feelings subsided a little, he asked, "Where is that rehabilitation centre? I will take him there."

Just as if waiting for the cue, Lorenzo started coughing in retaliation from the room next-door. They waited for a while before resuming their conversation.

"You know he might not take it nicely", said Lorenzo, "I do not think he is ready to admit that he even has a problem."

Bouki did not say anything but he looked terribly sad about the situation. He knew that it might take a while to convince his friend about going for help but he was ready to do everything to make things better for his friend.

"We will convince him, right?", said Bouki, "You and me. We are his friends after all."

George Beret smiled at the innocent man sitting in front of him.

It was getting rather late and since there was no way to carry the sleeping Lorenzo all the place to his apartment, George asked them to stay over for the night.

"One thing more", said George as they were about to retire to their rooms for the night, "Let me talk to him on this subject."

—

George Beret's request from the previous night had caused quite a lot of mental stress to Bouki. He was unsure why George had made this request. He was having doubts on the matter, as he could not understand why George thought himself to be a better option to have this discussion with Lorenzo. After pondering over the problem for the whole night, he decided he knew the answer to the question to some extent.

I think I am too emotionally involved with my friend and this discussion needs a more logical argument to convince Lorenzo.

That made a lot of sense to him and he decided to let George take care of the matter. Initially, they thought that conducting the plan in a way to keep it from Lorenzo would be difficult but it proved to be a rather easy matter since most of the time, their friend was too drunk to know what they were doing. After careful discussion, they decided how Lorenzo should be approached on the subject. It took them a week to do all that and when they finally spoke to him, it was a shock to see him being so open to the idea.

Bouki was shocked, because in the past years, ever since his friend had started drinking heavily, every time he had decided to approach the subject, Lorenzo had never been open to the idea. Yet, suddenly he was ready to go to a rehabilitation centre with them. Bouki could tell something was fishy but he could not put his finger on the real problem.

Yet, he decided to be happy that at least his friend was ready for it. Had he known what was cooking between his other two friends; he would not have been so happy!

The job at the "Amazonian Expedition" was just a matter of routine. However, one day Mr. Ventura came to Bouki and told him that he would have to go to Machu Picchu for a week. Their company was considering a coalition with another tourism agency at Peru and a team was being sent there to meet the representatives of that company. Mr. Ventura trusted Bouki a lot and he had confidence in his negotiation and communication skills as well. Therefore, he had decided to send him as the leader of the team. Bouki loved traveling. In fact, it was Lorenzo's love of roaming around that had first ignited a desire in him to travel as well. He had automatically assumed that Lorenzo would go with him as well. However, it came as quite a shock when Lorenzo told him that he was not in the team. What really hurt, however, was Lorenzo's decision to go for the rehabilitation process in the week that he was leaving for Peru.

Yet, he could not muster the courage to tell Lorenzo to wait for the next week. What if he changed his mind? thoughtBouki. For him, it was enough that his friend was ready to work on his bad habit of alcoholism. He decided to not say anything on the matter now, especially to Lorenzo. George, however, was an altogether different story.

Bouki would not stop instructing him on how to treat his friend. George proved to be a nice man and tried his best not to get irritated by Bouki's annoying behavior. He listened to everything with patience and told him that he would take great care of Lorenzo. It was the same talk they had every time they met—Bouki with his concerns and fears, George Beret with his words of solace.

Finally, the day arrived when Bouki left for Peru. He said goodbye to both his friends with a heavy heart. It was clear that he wanted to accompany his friend on his difficult journey but there was no way for him to do so.

"It is only your first visit there", he kept telling Lorenzo, "The next time you will have to go there, I will be with you. This is just a visit to get to know things. They won't admit you right away."

Lorenzo gave no reply. For some reason, he looked hurt but Bouki had no idea why would that be. Such disheartening behavior from his friend was hurting him as well. Unsure about how to respond to this, he glanced at George, who was standing right next to Lorenzo.

"Bouki, they might admit him right away. You know his condition is serious. You would not want them to wait if you know what is good for our friend here. Would you?", said George Beret.

Bouki had no choice but to accept the situation. What was the point of waiting anyway?, he thought. He went to Peru with a heavy heart. For one week, he had no contact with his friends and it caused him great stress. He wanted to know what was happening in Sao Paulo and most of all he wanted to know what were the opinions of the doctors and therapists at the rehabilitation center about Lorenzo's case. However, there was no way for him to contact with anybody.

He only got a small chance to talk to Mr. Ventura on the first day but nothing more. He had told him that both his friends were fine and had headed for the rehabilitation center but since it was situated in a village, there was no way of establishing any contact. The week passed in depression.

Apart from his concerns about his friend, Bouki was also homesick. He wanted to wind up the business meeting as soon as possible and return home. There was no point in traveling around if you did not have suitable companionship to enjoy the visits with you. He had finally learnt it the hard way. He yearned for the company of his friends. Whenever he would find a nice place, he wanted to appreciate it by talking about it to his friends. Not finding Lorenzo with him only made him sadder and he would not be able to enjoy the place and atmosphere either.

Although he wanted to return to Sao Paulo as soon as possible, it still took him a week to wind up the whole business. The day he was to board the plane back home, he could not help but smile. The turmoil of the past week was something he did not want to experience in his life ever. It was not only the pain of knowing that his friend was hurting and needed him but it was also about the strange behavior Lorenzo had had towards him. He had been thinking throughout the time he had spent alone in Peru about what wrong he had actually done towards his friend to deserve such behavior.

May be it was because I had been pressurizing him a lot, unnecessarily, he thought, or was it because I had shouted at him that night.

There were a lot of things bothering him and he was trying to figure out the reasons behind everything that had been happening lately in their lives. Unfortunately, even after giving it considerable thought, he was not able to figure out why Lorenzo had acted so withdrawn. Most of all, he wanted to know the cause of that expression Lorenzo had when Bouki had tried to tell him that the next time he would definitely go with him to the rehabilitation center.

He was now on his plane with his team. They were returning to Sao Paulo and Bouki was extremely happy about it. He was sure that whatever happened, at the end of this journey, he would have all his answers. He was at least right about that. He got the answers alright.

—

Instead of going to the office or the apartment, he went straight to George Beret's house. It was 6:00 P.M. and Bouki was sure that George would be home. However, he was surprised when George's cook told him that he was not home. He asked him several other questions to figure out where his friend was but the cook had no idea. Next, he went to Mr. Ventura's bungalow. Another surprise was waiting for him in the form of Mr. Ventura's absence. He had no idea what to do so he decided to call Lorenzo.

Where all of them have gone, he thought to himself. This sudden vanishing of his friends turned even more annoying when he realized that Lorenzo's cell phone was switched off. Despair took over him and then he finally dialed George Beret's number. After two or three bells, the businessman attended the call.

This call lasted only a minute but that one minute was enough to create an abyss in Bouki's life. It was a hole that nothing in the world would fill. He knew it and before he could figure out what should be done, he found himself losing consciousness. His friendship with Lorenzo Augusto had ended. Lorenzo Augusto was dead!

Chapter 10

Moving to Rio de Janeiro

Lorenzo had had lung cancer and it had been at the final stage. Lorenzo had found about it 2 years ago. He had tried his best to find a cure for it but there was nothing that could be done. While the situation was too much for the poor man to handle on his own, he could simply not bring himself to admit the truth in front of his dear friend. He could not see Bouki heartbroken. Therefore, he had decided to keep it a secret. However, it was impossible for him to bear the pain alone and so when he found a good friend in the form of George, he decided to let him in the secret as well.

George Beret was the perfect candidate in this situation according to Lorenzo. He cared for him but not as much as Bouki did. He was sympathetic and caring. Lorenzo knew that he could tell him his secret and ask for his help without causing him eternal damage. He also knew that this man's decency was enough to keep his secret. He knew he could trust George to not tell his secret to his best friend. This was the reason why

Lorenzo could not bear to be in Bouki's company anymore. He knew that Bouki had seen a lot in his life already and this would be an enormous blow to him.

"He cared for me, right", Bouki was shouting, "That was why he was considerate enough to die on me while all this time being a jerk to me."

George was now free to tell Bouki all the secrets of his dear friend and there was no job he had regretted doing more than he was regretting this. Watching a man in his mid-fifties breaking down like that was heart wrenching. Even Bouki was surprised at his own emotions. When his wife and daughter had died, he had shut himself in a cocoon and now he was shouting like a two-year-old kid.

"I am not justifying Lorenzo's actions, Bouki", said George, "However, it was my duty to honor the wishes of a dying man."

"All that drinking was killing him faster but since he was dying already he did not care for the consequences of his actions anymore", Bouki was trying to make sense of all that had happened. "This was why he did not care what would happen to me after he was gone."

"Please do not be like this", said George, "You know very well that Lorenzo's intentions were not as evil as you are making them out to be. I know you are in pain but so was he and he cared for you more than he cared for his life. Do not ruin the memories of a friendship that was so great."This silenced the old man for a while and George found it to be the perfect chance to talk more sense into Bouki. "I know my saying this would not make your suffering easier but I want you to be glad that it happened."

George's words were finally making sense to the grief stricken man. He decided to look into his friend's eyes. At some level, they understood each other and Bouki realized as he observed the dark circles under George's classic Caucasian eyes that this man had been suffering as well. He was not without emotions either and he loved the departed as well. That was when he knew they must now take care of each other.

Apparently, George Beret had been thinking the same thing.

"Come with me", said George Beret.

"Where?" asked Bouki.

"Rio de Janeiro", replied George Beret.

Without further ado, Bouki decided to accompany George.

Chapter 11

FIFA World Cup, 2014

The grief that had gripped poor Bouki was indeed deep but after spending so many years in the world, he had finally understood that there was no way to stay safe from being hurt. He had met many people who claimed to have their hard shells on, that protected them from heartbreak since they had the capacity to keep themselves from being attached to people and emotions. Bouki, however, was not like that. He was a man of feelings and he knew that. He would rather get hurt than stop living. All his years of experiencing life had taught him that being vulnerable might hurt but you could neither give nor receive love without being vulnerable. Bouki preferred to love!

Now that he was in a hurting phase, he knew how to tackle it as well. He knew that he would have to must busy himself with work and anything that might come his way. That was the main reason why he had accepted George Beret's offer in the first place. While it was hard saying his goodbyes to everyone at the "Amazonian Expedition", especially Mr. Ventura, but Bouki knew that standing water always ended up smelling foul. He needed to get out his comfort zone and live a different life. Three years were a lot of time and Lorenzo had been his only inspiration all that time. Now he was ready to write the end of that story. He knew that it would always belong to him since he had been a part of it but there was no point in dragging it when Fate had ended it already. Amidst such feelings, he left for his new destination.

With the end of September, the year 2013 entered its last trimester. George had already briefed Bouki about the significance of this period. The Football World Cup in 2014 was to be held in Brazil and George was ready to take as much advantage from this situation as was possible. The Brazilian government was taking the matter extremely seriously and the cost designated to make this a success had been higher than had been ever expended in the history of football world cups. A major part of the cost was to be spent on the infrastructure and the stadium. A number of construction projects were planned for facilitating the hosting of the grand world cup. George knew that it was a great time to make the most out of his business and Bouki agreed. For the next 6 months, Bouki was busy.

Bouki and George Beret worked day in and day out to be a part of the various construction projects that were to be conducted. The results were also mind blowing not only in terms of success but also in terms of money. Their efforts were not wasted and they definitely did not go unappreciated. In fact, George's company reached new heights of recognition and fame.

Yet, Bouki was not satisfied. He had a lot of money in his pocket and he had grown to love George. Moreover, he was given the chance to roam around all over Brazil but somehow it was not enough for him. He knew he needed more and so did George Beret.

There was no way to keep Mr. Ti Juan Bouki in confinement. He had always been a free spirit and there was no way to keep him chained. No matter how much Beret wanted him to stay; there was nothing he could do to stop him. Bouki was only looking for a way out.

Although he did find a way to get away from the country, it was not in a manner he had been looking forward to.

After the world cup ended and Bouki realized what kind of fortune he had made, he decided to go for a world tour. However, the money was still not enough for him to enjoy the trip to the full extent. He had to at least work for 2.5 more years to take that trip with full luxury. He talked about that to George Beret and he agreed with Bouki.

"I think you are right, my friend", said George, "The kind of trip you are looking for requires you to earn some more fortune."

"I know", said Bouki, "I am heavily indebted to you George."

George Beret smiled knowingly but said, "Why do you say that, Bouki?"

"All this money", replied Bouki, "I would never have dreamt of attaining this kind of money. I mean, don't get me wrong, I am definitely not a money worshipper but I had always had some dreams and for fulfilling them, I needed a huge amount of money with me."

"And", replied George Beret, "You never thought it would be possible for you to get your hands on that kind of money?"

Bouki simply nodded.

"Bouki", thus began George Beret, "All the money sitting in your bank account is a result of your own efforts and hard work. I do not understand your humility. I might have given you the opportunity to use your hidden talents but they had always been there inside you. You were doing pretty great at Amazonian Expedition as well but that was a sector that was not paying you much. I am pretty sure that if you would go for something better than this, you would be on top of that as well."

This little speech was enough to bring tears of joy in Bouki's eyes. He had no words to appreciate what George Beret had done for him so he just went over to him and hugged him. The gesture was so authentic that it even moved the rather immovable George Beret.

In order to deal with his emotions and handle all the awkwardness in a dignified manner, George Beret continued with his speech.

"Besides, I think that we have been missing a lot on the fun here. We have been so busy with the official work and holding meetings that even though we have been doing a lot of traveling, we were never really able to appreciate any of the places. How about the two of us just appreciate the beauty of Rio de Janeiro?"

Bouki smiled. He liked the idea and it was exactly the kind of thing he would have done with Lorenzo. He missed his old friend but time was healing the pains of his past. Yet, he knew nothing could completely clear his slate. There had been too many things on his plate. He still remembered and missed his wife and daughter. Some things never change…

"Let's do it", said Bouki, "I mean it is an awesome idea. In fact, this one is even better than your idea of investing in the world cup business."

Both of them laughed at this. Life, for Bouki, was getting back on track.

Chapter 12

Making Traveling Plans

Bouki and George went on a fun rampage. From breathtaking beaches to beautiful tropical landscapes, they did not leave anything when it came to exploring the city. They became really great friends, as with every passing day, they stayed together and got the chance to know each other better. They kept on developing their friendship over the coming years as well. Two years of friendship later, in the year of 2016, Mrs. George Beret decided to visit her husband. She was not alone though. Her children and two cousins were with her.

For Bouki, it was an honor to meet the wife of one of his two best friends. Soon, he had fallen in love with his friend's children. The daughter's name was Lydia and she was around the age of his own Rose when the earthquake had robbed him of her. He treated her like his own daughter and the little son was only 8 or so years old and Bouki loved playing with him as if he would have played with his grandson. It was at times like this that the full extent of his loss would hit him, making him extremely sad.

Soon, the desire to run away from this place started disturbing him again. He started finding himself restless, as he was ready to run away from this city and country as well. One thing led to another and soon he found himself discussing the issue with his friend once again. As if that was not enough, this time Mrs. Beret's cousins were also there.

"I want to go for that world trip, George", said Bouki, his voice was a mixture of excitement and despair, "I do not want to waste anymore life. I do not even know how much time I have. I am 56 years old and some of my body parts and organs are not functioning as they once used to do. There are times when I fail to enjoy an experience as much as I should. I do not want to miss out on life. Lorenzo wanted me to travel too."

The desperation in his voice and the longing to visit the unknown places in the world was indeed enough to soften anyone's heart. Therefore, even before George could make a reply, Mrs. Beret's cousins, who were brothers and were there on some business of their own, suggested that the three of them should go together.

While George Beret was not in favor of this idea, Bouki thought it was only because he did not want Bouki to leave him. When Bouki showed high level of interest in the proposition, George decided to back down.

Mrs. Beret's cousins were called John and William Derek. They were rather different in appearances but they always agreed on every matter. John was tall and dark with a solemn expression always plastered on his face, while Will was rather short and he was always smiling. However, it was always John who made the decisions and Will just agreed with all of his brother's suggestions. It was as if he did not have a mind of his own. This was exactly what happened this time as well.

John came up with the idea that they should leave for America via a long route that would give them a chance to see other places on the way. Moreover, he said he knew a few people who could take care of the financial issues as well since Bouki was still a little short on that front.

The idea was received with high level of admiration. Almost all of them were happy about it except for George. He was a sensible man and already sensed that there was something fishy about the whole business. He knew for sure that in this world, nothing happens for free. Since everything comes at a cost, the people that his brother in law was referring to must be offering the help at some cost. However, when he tried to find the reason behind this favor and tried talking to John, he was not clear on the topic at all. When George's suspicions increased, he decided to talk Bouki out of it. He asked him to accompany him to the study alone for he wanted to discuss the matter in private.

"Bouki, I really think that you should wait for a while before going on this journey of yours", said George Beret to the one person he had come to love in spite of himself. It was in the last two year that he had realized that he had never had a friendship like that before. It was not even like that with Lorenzo. In that case, it had only been sympathy but here it was more than that—here it was love and friendship, care and good will.

Somehow, for the first time, Bouki was not ready to heed the advice of a good friend. He wanted to know why George was being so unsure about everything.

"What is wrong with you, George?",Bouki asked his friend, "You know I am not a child. I know what is good for me and what is not."

This behavior of his friend was hurtful for George and his broken feelings could be witnessed on his face. This softened poor Bouki a bit.

"I am sorry, George", he said after a minute's pause that was pregnant with tension and awkwardness, "I just want to do this. Even if there is a risk involved, I do not mind taking it. I am pretty sure I do not have much time left. I do not want to waste my life without doing it even if it means a huge risk. Do you understand what I am trying to say here?"

Unfortunately, George understood. He knew that there was no point in trying to change the mind of this adamant man. It was only sensible to let go of this situation here. So he smiled as a good friend would smile when his friend was about to make a mistake from his point of view and yet there was no way to stop him.

With all his money at stake, Uncle Bouki from Aquin, Haiti, decided to go to America.

Chapter 13

America—Here I Come

All the planning had been done by John Derek while Bouki and Will just sat there as spectators. The people that John had been referring to were some of his old friends and George was extremely suspicious about them. He knew that John had once been to the jail because of some minor crime. He had been a child then and had been in custody for only a few months. Yet, when he had came out of there, he was a changed man. Nobody was quite sure what happened with him in there but he had made these strange friends in there, which were still with him. George suspected that it was these friends of his that were involved in planning their travel right now. Yet, he knew there was no point in asking because John had always been able to tackle that topic with tact. Also, George did not want to look desperate in Bouki's eyes. He wanted to let him go. He wanted Bouki to fly.

The plan was simple. They were following the age-old route to reach America. First, they would go to Ecuador, then Peru. From there, they would move to Columbia, then Mexico and finally to the American border. George could tell that this was nothing but illegal entrance in America, and yet, there was no punt in trying to explain this to Bouki. He was keen to take all the risks involved.

After waiting for a few months, they were ready to leave for their journey. Bouki had packed a few books with him as well. He had a peculiar condition where he could only read while traveling. Therefore, he had completed most of his readings while he had been on the move. Sometimes, he wondered if that was the reason why he loved traveling so much in the first place.

As it so happened, when they were leaving for their journey to America, something huge was about to change for that country. Something or rather someone was at work that was going to shake the essence of a country that had, hitherto, been a symbol of freedom. The brave new world was going to change and Bouki was about to find himself in the midst of the chaos that was about to ensue.

It was November 2016 and the people of America were about to make the biggest mistake of their lives. It was a mistake with consequences running too far and too wide. Something terrible was about to happen.

Bouki and his friends were, however, oblivious to that as they had started on their journey already. While they had been following politics until now and were hopeful that the lady would save the day, they lost all sense of time as they were jammed into a series of trucks, ships, and various other vehicles in their journey. They also could not care less about what was happening in American politics since their sole focus was now on surviving the harsh conditions in which they had been thrown.

Bouki was only beginning to realize the horrors of his decision. The traveling conditions were nothing as John had described. For several days, they were locked in the back of trucks. They had their instructions to sit inside as still as was possible. They were only given food at specific intervals and there were specific spots where they were allowed to come out of their hiding place for relieving themselves. It took Bouki a few days to realize that he was only left with one backpack that contained his documents, books, and two pieces of clothing. He, like the other passengers accompanying him, had been robbed of all their other belongings. There was no point in arguing because they were passing through unknown lands illegally and anybody who tried to create any kind of trouble was left alone then and there.

Bouki began to hate John for doing this to him but the man was nowhere to be seen now. In the first few days, John and Will were seen traveling with them but they always sat in the front seats of the vehicles and there was only minimal contact between Bouki and them. In fact, he realized that the brothers were ignoring him on purpose for once, when he tried to catch Will's attention, he had simply looked helpless as his brother shoved him away from Bouki's line of vision.

While Bouki was enraged to see this kind of behavior, there was nothing he could do. He finally found solace in his books. His favorite one was "The Hobbit." He found the fantastic adventures of Bilbo extremely relatable. At least it was relaxing to know that other people had been on trips like that as well and he was not the first one to venture on something like this on a whim.

Bilbo is a fictional character, Bouki, he thought and yet he was a staunch believer that there was not much of a difference between fiction and reality. It was only that we read about the one while the other is experienced by us and therefore, we find the latter to be harder while the former is a source of pleasure for us. Man is sadist, he thought, as long as it comes at the expense of another person's pains, man loves misery.

Bouki realized that he was turning into a hopeless man. With every country they reached, Bouki found himself losing hope and turning into a sadist. He knew this would not do. He was not the person he had always taught himself to be. He knew he had to change himself for the better.

They were in Mexico, when the results were announced—Donald Trump was elected the 45th President of the United States of America. Things were definitely not looking good!

While the distance between them and their final destination was not much, they were supposed to wait a few days before making their final move. They were told to come out of their hiding from the back of the trucks they had last been traveling in. They were now to take showers, clean themselves up, and change clothes. Uncle Bouki was given a new pair of trousers and shirt. He was sent along with the rest of his companions from the adventure to a salon to have their beards shaved and trimmed as per their desire. Bouki had decided to let go of every strand on his head as well as his face. He was bald now.

Self-actualization, he thought as he smiled. He could remember someone telling him about that concept when he was a young boy. It was all hazy now and came in parts only. It was such a long time ago when he had his innocence with him, when he knew he could trust the people around him. Now standing in a foreign land, in the company of a group of strangers, feeling cheated and betrayed, he knew he had changed. The journey had been tough, he had learnt a lot, and yet he was broken.

Uncle Bouki knew that it would take him some time to heal but he was equally sure that he would always have his baggage—a few open wounds hurting time and again and sometimes a little blood trickling down from them. He was human and he knew that contentment and happiness were not the fuels that had him going. It was perhaps the pain and misery that came with the curse of being sensitive and hopeful.

He wanted to jerk these thoughts away from his mind but he was not really in control. He hated hope—the miserable and pathetic miss, who looked beautiful on the surface but once you got to know her, she eluded you in the most elaborate way possible. It is always her archenemy—despair, that came to save you—the savior!

Despite all his bitterness, Bouki could feel a ray of hope shining inside his heavy heart. Soon they would be in America—the new world! What was better than getting a chance to start over your life in such a splendid country? While he knew that his pockets were completely empty, he also had enough confidence in himself. He knew he would make himself useful in one way or the other and his hard work would pay off as it had always done. He knew his dedication could save him from poverty. Moreover, he had more faith in the new country. America, in his mind, had always been etched as a symbol of freedom and equality. After going through so much, he had lost almost all hope of ever reaching that land of his dreams and yet he was only days away from his destination.

—

Everything after that seemed like a dream to him. He boarded another vehicle and saw the doors being shut on him. He was engulfed in darkness once more and yet there was light inside him. He could almost bring himself to smile a little as he shared the thrilled atmosphere of his vehicle. The other men were glad too that their long journey was about to come to an end.

Minutes turned into hours and hours into days. Soon, Uncle Bouki was ordered to come out into the day light. They had reached the place they had been looking forward to. They were to cross the border to El Paso and that was to be the end of their journey.

After going through so much, Uncle Bouki had finally reached America!

Chapter 14

There is no ending to Bouki's Troubles

When Bouki was told to cross the border with a few of the other men who were accompanying him, he realized that his challenges had not come to an end yet. He was sent with a company of other old men because they could be put at risk, as they were all old. The managers had decided that it was safe to run the risk with them.

While Bouki had his documents with him, even he knew that they were not of much use if he was caught because he had finally realized that they were not traveling legally. He wanted to protest against this partiality but he did not have the energy of being put to any further tests. He was malnourished and a few meals he had been given in Mexico had not been enough to compensate for the harsh treatment he had been receiving for several of the past months. He could not bring himself to have any kind of argument with anybody at that moment.

If you would look at the scene from afar instead of through Bouki's vision, you could see a row of old men inching their way to the border. From afar, the scene almost looked as if a line of ants was returning home after a long journey but their postures were not relaxed, as they should have been if they were returning home. They looked more as if they were on a mission they already knew would be of no use at all.

Knowing that they were doing the thing illegally, Bouki knew somewhere in his subconscious that it should have been done at night so there would be only a little proof of the mysterious activity. However, it was not the case and they were told to make their move in the middle of the day. Apparently, their leaders had talked to and bribed the people who were in charge of the border at that time of the day. They were supposed to be out of harm's way but Bouki's troubles were only far from over at this point of his life. He still had a lot to face and experience.

"Where do you think you old men are going?" a harsh voice came from the shadows. Bouki was surprised at first and then a familiar feeling of doom clouded him. He knew for sure that something was wrong and he knew that soon the façade that had been woven by the two Derek brothers would come crumbling down right to its bottom and Bouki knew he would somehow be found buried beneath the mess. Unfortunately, Uncle Bouki's suspicions were right…

"We are going to America", replied someone from their company and his reply was welcomed by a roar of skeptic laughter. Uncle Bouki realized that he had never hated any sound more than that laughter. He tried to see what the man from the shadows was like but even after squinting a great deal, he failed to make out any detectable figure.

The rest of that evening was spent in a blur. He heard a lot of words and that was when he found himself realizing the ugliness of such loathsome terminologies such as illegal, foreigners, immigrants, and refugees. The Trump government was definitely not ready to welcome people like Uncle Bouki. After going through a lot of rude behavior, insults, and humiliation, Uncle Bouki was sent to jail.

Thus began Uncle Bouki's time in American jail. He saw a life that was harder than he had ever imagined. He was getting older day after day and his bones were losing interest in continuing their daily functioning as well. Yet he was alive. He had heard from his grandmother that it was a rule of nature that the older a person got; the more he started to love his life. May be that was what had happened to him as all his thoughts and energy were obsessed with the idea of survival. He wanted to live through thick and thin.

His life at the jail was another era that helped him in refining his thinking abilities. Initially, he found it rather tough to accept the solitary mode of life; since in his mind, he had accepted that the people here were mean. He also only encountered such souls in the jail. Yet that phase was only temporary and with the passage of time, he found himself accepting even this life as well.

It was ironic that even though he was in America and he was working with all his might, he was only given the minimum—food, shelter, and clothing. Soon, he found ways to earn some money despite the difficulties. Moreover, he found books and for the first time in his life, he did not have to travel to immerse himself in good books. The bibliophile in him was now fully awake and did not need the movements of a vehicle to trigger his love for words. He would read like a maniac.

The jailers were astonished to see a foreigner man being so keen on reading literature. That was one of the few things that allowed him to keep his sanity. The adventures he read about in the books were enough to keep his soul nourished. He found his mind opening as new ideas began to penetrate his skull. Ti Jan Bouki, who had always believed in hard work, was finally beginning to accept that Fate was for real and some events were to happen no matter what! There was nothing that could be done to have the situation changed. For no matter how hard you try, you would always find that it is impossible to change the course of action.

It had taken Bouki a lot of traveling, reading, pains, losses, and life changing experiences to come to terms with the reality. In the depths of darkness, he had finally found and learnt something new—there was no point in crying for nothing. Life is hard and it is what it is!

Chapter 15

Deported!

Uncle Bouki stayed in jail for three months. His good behavior and love for reading were the two major reasons that he was allowed to go off easy. The others who were caught with him had not been so cooperative as Bouki. While all of them had said bad things about the country and its damaging policies, there was even one person who had tried to escape the jail altogether. Bouki had no idea what was to happen to him but he knew that it could not be good.

Bouki, on the other hand, was rather glad when the court ordered him to be deported back to his country—Haiti!

He had finally realized how much he had been missing his country. He had spent enough time wandering around aimlessly and it was high time for him to return and invest in his own country.

As if I have anything left to invest, Bouki thought patronizingly. He was robbed of his money by George Beret's brothers-in-law. Once in jail, he had had the chance of meeting one of his traveling companions. The first thing he asked from him was what happened to the two fraudulent brothers. The answer he had received made his blood boil. The two of them had managed to cross the border along with the rest of the party. In fact, they had known in advance that an officer was hiding to catch their party so they had sent Bouki and the other elderly as escape goat. While the officer and his party were busy dealing with Bouki and his companions, the others took another route and crossed the border.

"Bastards!" exclaimed had Bouki.

He had cooled off now. His past year had been so full of pain and challenges that he has somehow learnt to let go of things. He knew now that the past could not hurt you unless you wanted it to. Uncle Bouki did not want anything to hurt him anytime soon.

What does it matters if I do not have much money on me at the moment, he thought to himself, For one day I will have money. As long as my intentions are good and clear, I know there is nothing I should be afraid of or allow to hinder my plans.

Such were his thoughts as he left for his country. He could feel himself completing the circle, returning to the point he had first started at. From Haiti to Haiti! He was planning to accept his country and utilize his talents and expertise to do something better for it.

He was an altered man, he thought. There was one more thing he was planning to do, the moment he landed on his country's soil and that was contacting his dearest friend George Beret. There had been no contact between them ever since he had left George's house at Rio de Janeiro and it was around 3 to 4 months ago. While he had wanted to meet him once before leaving for his country, he knew there was no way it was possible and yet he longed to see George's face.

His flight back to Haiti was uneventful. When he reached Aquin, there had been several apprehensions in his mind. He was not sure how much his birthplace would have changed. Moreover, he was rather scared. He did not want to be reminded of the earthquake and its causalities once again. Most of all, he did not want to miss his family and yet he knew that achieving the last feat was near to impossible. As long as he was alive, that feeling of loss would always be there to accompany him.

He wanted to make a call to his friend George Beret but when he put his hands in his pocket to retrieve the money, he realized that he only had $5 on him—one more gift of humiliation from the US government.

With a tinge of pain, he realized that it was all the money he had since he had sold all of his property before he had left for Brazil. Somehow, he found in him the courage to laugh at this rather hurting situation. There he was standing in the middle of nowhere with only $5 in the pockets of his trousers. Even his clothes were a charity from the US government. The realization hit him hard and made him feel quite bad. It was right at that moment when one of his subordinates from the days when he was a Major in this city, recognized him.

Ti Jan Bouki was surprised to see this young man remember him. It had been a long time ago that they must have worked together. In any case, Bouki's appearance had changed a great deal. His eyes were not big and shiny but drooping eyelids gave him a tired look. He had developed a hunchback and he was hairless to the point of looking freaky. Yet this man had only taken a minute to recognize his old leader.

"Sir, you are back" he said with enthusiasm, "Where are you living nowadays?"

Before Bouki could answer, the young man came up with a number of other questions as well.

"When did you come anyway?" asked the young man, "Please stay at my home if you would not mind, that is."

"I would never mind being with an old friend."

This brought a smile on the young man's face and then he said, "A lot has changed since you had left the place, Sir. You will notice it eventually. By the way, the latest attraction of the area is the new club."

"What? A club here in our area?" asked Bouki in a surprised voice. They were advancing finally.

"Let me take you there, Sir", said the excited subordinate, "It may not be like the amazing clubs you would have seen there in the outside world, but it is good enough for us."

Bouki only smiled and nodded. He had no idea how to communicate his unfortunate series of adventures to this young man.

Chapter 16

The Borlette

When Bouki entered the club, he found it to be rather impressive. There was everything in there that a club should have. Uncle Bouki loved the music that was being played in there. He appreciated how it was not some loud noises but real Haitian music that he had grown up listening to. He was just catching up with the rhythm when he saw the lottery tickets being sold on one corner of the room. As if he had been looking for a way to test his luck ever since he had realized the importance of Fate, he grabbed the chance at once.

All he had was a $5 note on him. He did a little calculation and realized that he had around 345 gourdes. It seemed to him like a fair amount of money and he bought the lottery ticket. The result was to be announced the next day.

Bouki went home with his young friend. He was very excited about the whole business. Although he was not hopeful that he would actually win anything substantial, he was glad that he had not lost his sense of risk taking. He was so excited that he could hardly eat or sleep. His situation persisted until the moment the winner of the lottery was announced.

In The Bar, Bouki while watching TV, was taking two short of Barbancourt's rum grabbing the glass in one hand while in the other, he held the lottery ticket. Bouki looked up and saw an old man standing on the stage. He was wearing an expensive suit. He was holding on to a piece of paper as he kept talking in the mic. There were at least thousands of expectant faces looking at the man as if he had the answer to all their problems. It could have been true for the winner would have taken home a whooping amount of 10 million gourdes. That kind of money could address a lot if not all the problems of a man.

"01/12/10", the announcer said. It was after various years that Ti Jan Bouki found himself smiling and laughing.

—

Two years had passed since that fateful day had happened. Uncle Bouki was now an owner of a successful tourism company that had played a huge role in improving the country's image. A number of people work under him and serving his countrymen is what makes Uncle Bouki really happy and content.

Made in the USA
Columbia, SC
17 June 2025